EVOLUTION ISLAND

THEY TWINKLED LIKE JEWELS
PHILIP JOSÉ FARMER

EVOLUTION ISLAND

ISLAND

EDMOND HAMILTON

Jack Crane lay all morning in the vacant lot. Now and then he moved a little to quiet the protest of cramped muscles and stagnant blood, but most of the time he was as motionless as the heap of rags he resembled. Not once did he hear or see a Bohas agent, or, for that matter, anyone. The predawn darkness had hidden his panting flight from the transie jungle, his dodging across backyards while whistles shrilled and voices shouted, and his crawling on hands and knees down an alley into the high grass and bushes which fringed a hidden garden.

For a while his heart had knocked so loudly that he had been sure he would not be able to hear his pursuers if they did get close. It seemed inevitable that they would track him down. A buddy had told him that a new camp had just been built at a place only three hours drive away from the town. This meant that Bohas would be thick as hornets in the neighborhood. But no black uniforms had so far appeared. And then, lying there while the passionate and untiring sun mounted the sky, the bang-bang of his heart was replaced by a noiseless but painful movement in his stomach.

He munched a candy bar and two dried rolls which a housewife had given him the evening before. The tiger in his belly quit pacing back and forth; it crouched and licked its chops, but its tail was stuck up in his throat. Jack could feel the dry fur swabbing his pharynx and mouth. He suffered, but he was used to that. Night would come as surely as anything did. He'd get a drink then to quench his thirst.

Boredom began to sit on his eyelids. Just as he was about to accept some much needed sleep, he moved a leaf with an accidental jerk of his hand and uncovered a caterpillar. It was dark except for a row of yellow spots along the central line of some of its segments. As soon as it was exposed, it began slowly shimmying away. Before it had gone two feet, it was crossed by a moving shadow. Guiding the shadow was a black wasp with an orange ring around the abdomen. It closed the gap between itself and the worm with a swift, smooth movement and straddled the dark body.

Before the wasp could grasp the thick neck with its mandibles, the intended victim began rapidly rolling and unrolling and flinging itself from side to side. For a minute the delicate dancer above it could not succeed in clenching the neck. Its sharp jaws slid off the frenziedly jerking skin until the tiring creature paused for the chip of a second.

Seizing opportunity and larva at the same time, the wasp stood high on its legs and pulled the worm's front end from the ground, exposing the yellowed band of the underpart. The attacker's abdomen curved beneath its own body; the stinger jabbed between two segments of the prey's jointed length. Instantly, the writhing stilled. A shudder, and the caterpillar became as inert as if it were dead.

Jack had watched with an eye not completely clinical, feeling the sympathy of the hunted and the hounded for a fellow. His own struggles of the past few months had been as desperate, though not as hopeless, and ...

He stopped thinking. His heart again took up the rib-thudding. Out of the corner of his left eye he had seen a shadow that fell across the garden.

When he slowly turned his head to follow the stain upon the sun-splashed soil, he saw that it clung to a pair of shining black boots.

Jack did not say anything. What was the use? He put his hands against the weeds and pushed his body up. He looked into the silent mouth of a .38 automatic. It told him his running days were over. You didn't talk back to a mouth like that.

II

Jack was lucky. As one of the last to be herded into the truck, which had been once used for hauling cattle, he had more room to breathe than most of the others. He faced the rear bars. The vehicle was heading into the sun. Its rays were not as hard on him as on some of those who were so jam-packed they could not turn to get the hot yellow splotch out of their eyes.

He looked through lowered lids at the youths on either side of him. For the last three days in the transie jungle, the one standing on his left had given signs of what was coming upon him, what had come upon so many of the transies. The muttering, the indifference to food, not hearing you when you talked to him. And now the shock of being caught in the raid had speeded up what everybody had foreseen. He was hardened, like a concrete statue, into a half-crouch. His arms were held in front of him like a praying mantis', and his hands clutched a bar. Not even the pressure of the crowd could break his posture.

The man on Jack's right murmured something, but the roaring of motor and clashing of gears shifting on a hill squashed his voice. He spoke louder:

"*Cerea flexibilitas*. Extreme catatonic state. The fate of all of us."

"You're nuts," said Jack. "Not me. I'm no schizo, and I'm not going to become one."

As there was no reply, Jack decided he had not moved his lips enough to be heard clearly. Lately, even when it was quiet, people seemed to have trouble making out what he was saying. It made him mildly angry.

He shouted. It did not matter if he were overheard. That any of the prisoners were agents of the Bureau of Health and Sanity didn't seem likely.

Anyway, he didn't care. They wouldn't do anything to him they hadn't planned before this.

"Got any idea where we're going?"

"Sure. F.M.R.C. 3. Federal Male Rehabilitation Camp No. 3. I spent two weeks in the hills spying on it."

Jack looked the speaker over. Like all those in the truck, he wore a frayed shirt, a stained and torn coat, and greasy, dirty trousers. The black bristles on his face were long; the back of his neck was covered by thick curls. The brim of his dusty hat was pulled down low. Beneath its shadow his eyes roamed from side to side with the same fear that Jack knew was in his own eyes.

Hunger and sleepless nights had knobbed his cheekbones and honed his chin to a sharp point. An almost visible air clung to him, a hot aura that seemed to result from veins full of lava and eyeballs spilling out a heat that could not be held within him. He had the face every transie had, the face of a man who was either burning with fever or who had seen a vision.

Jack looked away to stare miserably at the dust boiling up behind the wheels, as if he could see projected against its yellow-brown screen his retreating past.

He spoke out of the side of his mouth. "What's happened to us? We should be happy and working at good jobs and sure about the future. We shouldn't be just bums, hobos, walkers of the streets, rod-hoppers, beggars, and thieves."

His friend shrugged and looked uneasily from the corners of his eyes. He was probably expecting the question they all asked sooner or later: *Why are you on the road?* They asked, but none replied with words that meant anything. They lied, and they didn't seem to take any pleasure in their lying. When they asked questions themselves, they knew they wouldn't get the truth. But something forced them to keep on trying anyway.

Jack's buddy evaded also. He said, "I read a magazine article by a Dr. Vespa, the head of the Bureau of Health and Sanity. He'd written the article just after the President created the Bureau. He viewed, quote, with alarm and apprehension, unquote, the fact that six percent of those between the ages of twelve and twenty-five were schizophrenics who needed institutionalizing. And he was, quote, appalled and horrified, unquote, that five percent of the nation were homeless unemployed and that three point seven percent of those were between the ages of fourteen and thirty. He said that if this schizophrenia kept on progressing, half the world would be in rehabilitation camps. But if that occurred, the sane half would go to pot. Back to the stone age. And the schizos would die."

*

He licked his lips as if he were tasting the figures and found them bitter.

"I was very interested by Vespa's reply to a mother who had written him," he went on. "Her daughter ended up in a Bohas camp for schizos, and her son had left his wonderful home and brilliant future to become a bum. She wanted to know why. Vespa took six long paragraphs to give six explanations, all equally valid and all advanced by equally distinguished sociologists. He himself favored the mass hysteria theory. But if you looked at his gobbledegook closely, you could reduce it to one phrase, *We don't know.*

"He did say this—though you won't like it—that the schizos and the transies were just two sides of the same coin. Both were infected with the same disease, whatever it was. And the transies usually ended up as schizos anyway. It just took them longer."

Gears shifted. The floor slanted. Jack was shoved hard against the rear boards by the weight of the other men. He didn't answer until the pressure had eased and his ribs were free to work for more than mere survival.

He said, "You're way off, schizo. My hitting the road has nothing to do with those split-heads. Nothing, you understand? There's nothing foggy or dreamy about me. I wouldn't be here with you guys if I hadn't been so interested in a wasp catching a caterpillar that I never saw the Bohas sneaking up on me."

While Jack described the little tragedy, the other allowed an understanding smile to bend his lips. He seemed engrossed, however, and when Jack had finished, he said:

"That was probably an ammophila wasp. *Sphex urnaria* Klug. Lovely, but vicious, little she-demon.

Injects the poison from her sting into the caterpillar's central nerve cord. That not only paralyzes but preserves it. The victim is always stowed away with another one in an underground burrow. The wasp attaches one of her eggs to the body of a worm. When the egg hatches, the grub eats both of the worms. They're alive, but they're completely helpless to resist while their guts are gnawed away. Beautiful idea, isn't it?

"It's a habit common to many of those little devils: *Sceliphron cementarium*, *Eumenes coarcta*, *Eumenes fraterna*, *Bembix spinolae*, *Pelopoeus* ..."

Jack's interest wandered. His informant was evidently one of those transies who spent long hours in the libraries. They were ready at the slightest chance to offer their encyclopaedic but often useless knowledge. Jack himself had abandoned his childhood bookwormishness. For the last three years his days and evenings had worn themselves out on the streets, passed in a parade of faces, flickered by in plate-glass windows of restaurants and department stores and business offices, while he hoped, hoped....

"Did you say you spied on the camp?" Jack interrupted the sonorous, almost chanting flow of Greek and Latin.

"Huh? Oh, yeah. For two weeks. I saw plenty of transies trucked in, but I never saw any taken out. Maybe they left in the rocket."

"Rocket?"

The youth was looking straight before him. His face was hard as bone, but his voice trembled.

"Yes. A big one. It landed and discharged about a dozen men."

"You nuts? There's been only one man-carrying rocket invented, and it lands by parachute."

"I saw it, I tell you. And I'm not so nutty I'm seeing things that aren't there. Not yet, anyway!"

"Maybe the government's got rockets it's not telling anybody about."

"Then what connection could there be between rehabilitation camps and rockets?"

Jack shrugged and said, "Your rocket story is fantastic."

"If somebody had told you four years ago that you'd be a bum hauled off to a concentration camp, you'd have said that was fantastic too."

Jack did not have time to reply. The truck stopped outside a high, barbed wire fence. The gate swung open; the truck bounced down the bumpy dirt road. Jack saw some black-uniformed Bohas seated by heavy machine guns. They halted at another entrance; more barbed wire was passed. Huge Dobermann pinschers looked at the transies with cold, steady eyes. The dust of another section of road swirled up before they squeaked to a standstill and the engine turned off.

This time, agents began to let down the back of the truck. They had to pry the pitiful schizo's fingers loose from the wood with a crow-bar and carry him off, still in his half-crouch.

A sergeant boomed orders. Stiff and stumbling, the transies jumped off the truck. They were swiftly lined up into squads and marched into the enclosure and from there into a huge black barracks. Within an hour each man was stripped, had his head shaven, was showered, given a grey uniform, and handed a tin plate and spoon and cup filled with beans and bread and hot coffee.

Afterwards, Jack wandered around, free to look at the sandy soil underfoot and barbed wire and the black uniforms of the sentries, and free to ask himself where, where, wherewherewhere? Twelve years ago it had been, but where, where, where, was...?

III

How easy it would have been to miss all this, if only he had obeyed his father. But Mr. Crane was so ineffectual....

"Jackie," he had said, "would you please go outside and play, or stay in some other room. It's very difficult to discuss business while you're whooping and screaming around, and I have a lot to discuss with Mr.—"

"Yes, Daddy," Jack said before his father mentioned his visitor's name. But he was not Jack Crane in his game; he was Uncas. The big chairs and the divan were trees in his imaginative eyes. The huge easy chair in which Daddy's caller (Jack thought of him only as "Mister") sat was a fallen log. He, Uncas, meant to hide behind it in ambush.

Mister did not bother him. He had smiled and said in a shrill voice that he thought Jack was a very nice boy. He wore a light grey-green Palm Beach suit and carried a big brown leather briefcase that looked too heavy for his soda straw-thin legs and arms. He was queer-looking because his waist was so narrow and his back so humped. And when he took off his tan Panama hat, a white fuzz exploded from his scalp. His face was pale as the moon in daylight. His broad smile showed teeth that Jack knew were false.

But the queerest thing about him was his thick spectacles, so heavily tinted with rose that Jack could not see the eyes behind them. The afternoon light seemed to bounce off the lenses in such a manner that no matter what angle you looked at them, you could not pierce them. And they curved to hide the sides of his eyes completely.

Mister had explained that he was an albino, and he needed the glasses to dim the glare on his eyes. Jack stopped being Uncas for a minute to listen. He had never seen an albino before, and, indeed, he did not know what one was.

"I don't mind the youngster," said Mister. "Let him play here if he wants to. He's developing his imagination, and he may be finding more stimuli in this front room than he could in all of outdoors. We should never cripple the fine gift of imagination in the young. Imagination, fancy, fantasy—or whatever you call it—is the essence and mainspring of those scientists, musicians, painters, and poets who amount to something in later life. They are adults who have remained youths."

Mister addressed Jack, "You're the Last of the Mohicans, and you're about to sneak up on the French captain and tomahawk him, aren't you?"

Jack blinked. He nodded his head. The opaque rose lenses set in Mister's face seemed to open a door into his naked grey skull.

The man said, "I want you to listen to me, Jack. You'll forget my name, which isn't important. But you will always remember me and my visit, won't you?"

Jack stared at the impenetrable lenses and nodded dumbly.

Mister turned to Jack's father. "Let his fancy grow. It is a necessary wish-fulfillment play. Like all human young who are good for anything at all, he is trying to find the lost door to the Garden of Eden. The history of the great poets and men-of-action is the history of the attempt to return to the realm that Adam lost, the forgotten Hesperides of the mind, the Avalon buried in our soul."

Mr. Crane put his fingertips together. "Yes?"

"Personally, I think that some day man will realize just what he is searching for and will invent a machine that will enable the child to project, just as a film throws an image on a screen, the visions in his psyche.

"I see you're interested," he continued. "You would be, naturally, since you're a professor of philosophy. Now, let's call the toy a specterscope, because through it the subject sees the spectres that haunt his unconscious. Ha! Ha! But how does it work? If you'll keep it to yourself, Mr. Crane, I'll tell you something: My native country's scientists have developed a rather simple device, though they haven't published anything about it in the scientific journals. Let me give you a brief explanation: Light strikes the retina of the eye; the rods and cones pass on impulses to the bipolar cells, which send them on to the optic nerve, which goes to the brain ..."

"Elementary and full of gaps," said Jack's father.

"Pardon me," said Mister. "A bare outline should be enough. You'll be able to fill in the details. Very well. This specterscope breaks up the light going into the eye in such a manner that the rods and cones receive only a certain wavelength. I can't tell you what it is, except that it's in the visual red. The scope also concentrates like a burning-glass and magnifies the power of the light.

"Result? A hitherto-undiscovered chemical in the visual purple of the rods is activated and stimulates the optic nerve in a way we had not guessed possible. An electrochemical stimulus then irritates the subconscious until it fully wakes up.

"Let me put it this way. The subconscious is not a matter of location but of organization. There are billions of possible connections between the neurons of the cortex. Look at those potentialities as so many cards in the same pack. Shuffle the cards one way and you have the common workaday *cogito, ergo sum* mind. Reshuffle them, and, bingo! you have the combination of neurons, or cards, of the unconscious. The specterscope does the redealing. When the subject gazes through it, he sees for the first time the full impact and result of his underground mind's workings in other perspectives than dreams or symbolical behavior. The subjective

Garden of Eden is resurrected. It is my contention that this specterscope will some day be available to all children.

"When that happens, Mr. Crane, you will understand that the world will profit from man's secret wishes. Earth will be a far better place. Paradise, sunken deep in every man, can be dredged out and set up again."

"I don't know," said Jack's father, stroking his chin thoughtfully with a finger. "Children like my son are too introverted as it is. Give them this psychological toy you suggest, and you would watch them grow, not into the outside world, but into themselves. They would fester. Man has been expelled from the Garden. His history is a long, painful climb toward something different. It is something that is probably better than the soft and flabby Golden Age. If man were to return, he would regress, become worse than static, become infantile or even embryonic. He would be smothered in the folds of his own dreams."

"Perhaps," said the salesman. "But I think you have a very unusual child here. He will go much farther than you may think. Why? Because he is sensitive and has an imagination that only needs the proper guidance. Too many children become mere bourgeois ciphers with paunches and round 'O' minds full of tripe. They'll stay on earth. That is, I mean they'll be stuck in the mud."

"You talk like no insurance salesman I've ever met."

"Like all those who really want to sell, I'm a born psychologist," Mister shrilled. "Actually, I have an advantage. I have a Ph.D. in psychology. I would prefer staying at home for laboratory work, but since I can help my starving children—I am not joking—so much more by coming to a foreign land and working at something that will put food in their mouths, I do it. I can't stand to see my little ones go hungry. Moreover," he said with a wave of his long-fingered hand, "this whole planet is really a lab that beats anything within four walls."

"You spoke of famine. Your accent—your name. You're a Greek, aren't you?"

"In a way," said Mister. "My name, translated, means gracious or kindly or well-meaning." His voice became brisker. "The translation is apropos.

I'm here to do you a service. Now, about these monthly premiums ..."

Jack shook himself and stepped out of the mold of fascination that Mister's glasses seemed to have poured around him. Uncas again, he crawled on all fours from chair to divan to stool to the fallen log which the adults thought was an easy chair. He stuck his head from behind it and sighted along the broomstick-musket at his father. He'd shoot that white man dead and then take his scalp. He giggled at that, because his father really didn't have any hairlock to take.

At that moment Mister decided to take off his specs and polish them with his breast-pocket handkerchief. While he answered one of Mr. Crane's questions, he let them dangle from his fingers. Accidentally, the lenses were level with Jack's gaze. One careless glance was enough to jerk his eyes back to them. One glance stunned him so that he could not at once understand that what he was seeing was not reality.

There was his father across the room. But it wasn't a room. It was a space outdoors under the low branch of a tree whose trunk was so big it was as wide as the wall had been. Nor was the Persian rug there. It was replaced by a close-cropped bright green grass. Here and there foot-high flowers with bright yellow petals tipped in scarlet swayed beneath an internal wind. Close to Mr. Crane's feet a white horse no larger than a fox terrier bit off the flaming end of a plant.

All those things were wonderful enough—but was that naked giant who sprawled upon a moss-covered boulder father? No! Yes! Though the features were no longer pinched and scored and pale, though they were glowing and tanned and smooth like a young athlete's they were his father's! Even the thick, curly hair that fell down over a wide forehead and the panther-muscled body could not hide his identity.

Though it tore at his nerves, and though he was afraid that once he looked away he would never again seize the vision, Jack ripped his gaze away from the rosy view.

The descent to the grey and rasping reality was so painful that tears ran down his cheeks, and he gasped as if struck in the pit of the stomach. How could beauty like that be all around him without his knowing it?

He felt that he had been blind all his life until this moment and would be forever eyeless again, an unbearable forever, if he did not look through the glass again.

He stole another hurried glance, and the pain in his heart and stomach went away, his insides became wrapped in a soft wind. He was lifted. He was floating, a pale red, velvety air caressed him and buoyed him.

He saw his mother run from around the tree. That should have seemed peculiar, because he had thought she was dead. But there she was, no longer flat-walking and coughing and thin and wax-skinned, but golden-brown and curvy and bouncy. She jumped at Daddy and gave him a long kiss. Daddy didn't seem to mind that she had no clothes on. Oh, it was so wonderful. Jack was drifting on a yielding and wine-tinted air and warmed with a wind that seemed to swell him out like a happy balloon....

Suddenly he was falling, hurtling helplessly and sickeningly through a void while a cold and drab blast gouged his skin and spun him around and around. The world he had always known shoved hard against him. Again he felt the blow in the solar plexus and saw the grey tentacles of the living reality reach for his heart.

Jack looked up at the stranger, who was just about to put his spectacles on the bridge of his long nose. His eyelids were closed. Jack never did see the pink eyes.

That didn't bother him. He had other things to think about. He crouched beside the chair while his brain tried to move again, tried to engulf a thought and failed because it could not become fluid enough to find the idea that would move his tongue to shriek, *No! No! No!*

And when the salesman rose and placed his papers in his case and patted Jack on the head and bent his opaque rose spectacles at him and said good-by and that he wouldn't be coming back because he was going out of town to stay, Jack was not able to move or say a thing. Nor for a long time after the door had closed could he break through the mass that gripped him like hardened lava. By then, no amount of screams and weeping would bring Mister back. All his father could do was to call a doctor who took the boy's temperature and gave him some pills.

IV

Jack stood inside the wire and bent his neck back to watch a huge black and silver oyster feel the dusk for a landing-field with its single white foot and its orange toes. Blindingly, lights sprang to attention over the camp.

When Jack had blinked his eyes back to normal, he could see over the flat half-mile between the fence and the ship. It lay quiet and glittering and smoking in the flood-beams. He could see the round door in its side swing open. Men began filing out. A truck rumbled across the plain and pulled up beside the metal bulk. A very tall man stepped out of the cab and halted upon the running board, from which he seemed to be greeting the newcomers or giving them instructions. Whatever he was saying took so long that Jack lost interest.

Lately, he had not been able to focus his mind for any length of time upon anything except that one event in the past. He wandered around and whipped glances at his comrades' faces, noting listlessly that their uniforms and shaved heads had improved their appearance. But nothing would be able to chill the feverishness of their eyes.

Whistles shrilled. Jack jumped. His heart beat faster. He felt as if the end of the quest were suddenly close. Somebody would be around the corner. In a minute that person would be facing him, and then ...

Then, he reflected, and sagged with a wave of disappointment at the thought, then there was nobody around the corner. It always happened that way. Besides, there weren't any corners in this camp. He had reached the wall at the end of the alley. Why didn't he stop looking?

Sergeants lined the prisoners up four abreast preparatory to marching them into the barracks. Jack supposed it was time to turn in for the night. He submitted to their barked orders and hard hands without resentment. They seemed a long way off. For the ten thousandth time he was thinking that this need not have happened.

If he had been man enough to grapple with himself, to wrestle as Jacob did with the angel and not let loose until he had felled the problem, he could be teaching philosophy in a quiet little college, as his father did. He had graduated from high school with only average marks, and then, instead of going to college, as his father had so much wanted him to, he had decided he would work a year. With his earnings, he would see the world.

He had seen it, but when his money ran out he had not returned home. He had drifted, taking jobs here and there, sleeping in flop-houses, jungles, park benches, and freight cars.

When the newly created Bureau of Health and Sanity had frozen jobs in an effort to solve the transiency problem, Jack had refused to work. He knew that he would not be able to quit a job without being arrested at once. Like hundreds of thousands of other youths, he had begged and stolen and hidden from the local police and the Bohas.

Even through all those years of misery and wandering, he had not once admitted to himself the true nature of this fog-cottoned grail. He knew it, and he did not know it. It was patrolling the edge of his mind, circling a far-off periphery, recognizable intake of breath.

"The plant-men!" he whispered, and Walton nodded, silently.

Together, and with a common horror, they watched the passing things. There seemed nothing human about the creatures under the bright moonlight. Mottled-green travesties on the human shape they seemed, masses of stringy fiber carelessly cast into a semi-human form. It was the faces of them that held Owen's gaze, blank expanses of smooth green in which the two eyes, circles of dead white, stood out dreadfully, staring and unwinking.

He had time only to note that the passing plant-men seemed to be carrying with them a number of large metal tools, or instruments, and then they had all gone by, and the two crouching men heard them shuffling down onto the beach and along the shore. For minutes they waited, listening, but no further sound came to them, so they rose and continued up the slope, doubly cautious after their unexpected encounter with the plant-men.

The moonlight made their progress easier now, and in a few minutes they stood on the very top of the ridge, from which they could survey nearly all the island's surface.

Instantly the attention of the two was riveted on the distant beaches at the island's eastern side, for there were lights there, masses of small, gleaming lights that came and went continually, moving about in swirls and eddies, like fireflies, and some of these were gathered into clusters here and there.

Along the distant beaches these lights were present for a distance of nearly two miles, and perhaps farther, since a rolling fold of the slope beneath them partly cut off their view in that direction. As they watched, a distant clangor of metal came to their ears from the direction of the lights, faint and far, a mighty hammering of metal on metal that came to their ears on the wings of a little breeze, then died away. They listened, and it came again, and again.

"The main camp of the plant-men," Walton whispered. "There must be thousands of them down there, judging from those lights."

"What are they doing, Walton?" asked Owen. "You heard that hammering? There's something big going on down there."

Walton nodded, watching the distant lights. "God knows that they're up to, down there. Whatever it is, Brilling is directing it, you may be sure. We can do nothing there, though." And he turned away from the east, and glanced around, then tugged at Owen's sleeve, pointing silently toward the northern end of the island.

A light was gleaming in that direction also, a steady unwinking beam that was nothing like the flitting illuminations in the east. "That light is from the cottage," Walton whispered. "That's our objective." And he started along the ridge toward the north.

Again Owen followed, and the two moved silently along the ridge toward the distant light, which, as they drew nearer, showed itself to be a square, lighted window. The ridge sloped down as they drew near the island's northern end, and in a few minutes they had come to within a half-mile of the stockade which enclosed the cottage and laboratory, and which lay down the slope a little below their present position.

Down they crept, until they could plainly see the cottage in by a crude silhouette but nameless. Any time he wanted to, he could have summoned it closer and said, *You are it, and I know you, and I know what I am looking for. It is...? Is what? Worthless? Foolish? Insane? A dream?*

Jack had never had the courage to take that action. When it seemed the thing was galloping closer, charging down upon him, he ran away. It must stay on the horizon, moving on, always moving, staying out of his grasp.

"All you guys, for'ard 'arch!"

Jack did not move. The truck from the rocket had come through a gate and stopped by the transies, and about fifty men were getting off the back.

The man behind Jack bumped into him. Jack paid him no attention. He did not move. He squinted at the group who had come from the rocket. They were very tall, hump-shouldered, and dressed in light grey-green Palm Beach suits and tan Panama hats. Each held a brown leather briefcase at the end of a long, thin arm. Each wore on the bridge of his long nose a pair of rose-colored glasses.

A cry broke hoarsely from the transies. Some of those in front of Jack fell to their knees as if a sudden poison had paralyzed their legs. They called names and stretched out open hands. A boy by Jack's side sprawled face-down on the sand while he uttered over and over again, "Mr. Pelopoeus! Mr. Pelopoeus!"

The name meant nothing to Jack. He did feel repulsed at seeing the fellow turn on his side, bend his neck forward, bring his clenched fists up against his chest, and jackknife his legs against his arms. He had seen it many times before in the transie jungles, but he had never gotten over the sickness it had first caused him.

He turned away and came almost nose to nose with one of the men from the rocket. He had put down his briefcase so it rested against his leg and taken a white handkerchief out of his breast pocket to wipe the dust from his lenses. His lids were squeezed shut as if he found the lights unbearable.

Jack stared and could not move while a name that the boy behind him had been crying out slowly worked its way through his consciousness. Suddenly, like the roar of a flashflood that is just rounding the bend of a dry gulch, the syllables struck him. He lunged forward and clutched at the spectacles in the man's hand. At the same time he yelled over and over the words that had filled out the blank in his memory.

"Mr. Eumenes! Mr. Eumenes!"

A sergeant cursed and slammed his fist into Jack's face. Jack fell down, flat on his back. Though his jaw felt as if it were torn loose from its hinge, he rolled over on his side, raised himself on his hands and knees, and began to get up to his feet.

"Stand still!" bellowed the sergeant. "Stay in formation or you'll get more of the same!"

Jack shook his head until it cleared. He crouched and held out his hands toward the man, but he did not move his feet. Over and over, half-chanting, half-crooning, he said, "Mr. Eumenes! The glasses! Please, Mr. Eumenes, the glasses!"

The forty-nine Mr. Eumenae-and-otherwise looked incuriously with impenetrable rosy eyes. The fiftieth put the white handkerchief back in his pocket. His mouth opened. False teeth gleamed. With his free hand he took off his hat and waved it at the crowd and bowed.

His tilted head showed a white fuzzlike hair that shot up over his pale scalp. His gestures were both comic and terrifying. The hat and the inclination of his body said far more than words could. They said, *Good-by forever, and bon voyage!*

Then Mr. Eumenes straightened up and opened his lids.

At first, the sockets looked as if they held no eyeballs, as if they were empty of all but shadows.

Jack saw them from a distance. Mr. Eumenes-or-his-twin was shooting away faster and faster and becoming smaller and smaller. No! He himself was. He was rocketing away within his own body. He was falling down a deep well.

He, Jack Crane, was a hollow shaft down which he slipped and screamed, away, away, from the world outside. It was like seeing from the wrong end of a pair of binoculars that lengthened and lengthened while the man with the long-sought-for treasure in his hand flew in the opposite direction as if he had been connected to the horizon by a rubber band and somebody had released it and he was flying towards it, away from Jack.

Even as this happened, as he knew vaguely that his muscles were locking into the posture of a beggar, hands out, pleading, face twisted into an the moonlight, a small, one-story affair, beside which was a long, low building that Owen knew to be the laboratory.

Walton jerked a finger toward the latter building. "The ray-projector is in there," he whispered, "and if you can get inside, remember that the reversing ray is turned on by the extreme left-hand switch. If we can just get into the laboratory! The gate of the stockade is open, and I don't see anyone around. Brilling is not using the ray-projector at all, now, for he turned off the accelerating ray after the plant-men were fully developed. But if we can sent out the reversing ray—"

Heart beating rapidly, Owen followed his friend, stealing down toward the open gate of the stockade. There was no sound or movement in the lighted cottage, nor in the clearing around the two buildings. His hopes ran high as they crept on.

Down, down, keeping as much as possible within the sheltering shadows, they went on, and now were passing through the open gate of the stockade, were moving soundlessly across the clearing toward the little laboratory building, whose open door beckoned to them like a magnet.

A hundred feet from that open door, Owen heard a sudden sound of running feet, and wheeling quickly, saw a little knot of dark shapes rushing through the stockade gate, toward Walton and himself. The plant-men!

"Walton!" he cried, and saw his friend turn swiftly. From one of the racing plant-men a burst of green fire suddenly sprang out toward the two men, barely grazing them. Before the deadly flame could be again thrown at them, a high, shrill call sounded from the cottage, a wailing scream flung toward the running plant-men like a command. Owen had a momentary glimpse of a strange, squat figure outlined against the door of the lighted cottage, then the mass of plant-men was pouring down on Walton and himself.

His automatic flashed into his hand and roared, once, twice, but the nearing plant-men rushed on, unhurt by the bullets that ripped through them. He heard a wail of utter despair from Walton, an exultant, shrill cry from the cottage, and then the plant-men had rushed down on him in a solid wave, knocking him from his feet. Something hard descended on Owen's head with stunning force, and as he sank to the ground, a great curtain of orange flame seemed to be unrolling itself in his brain. Then he felt himself falling, falling, tumbling down through bottomless depths of blackness and silence into complete unconsciousness.

5

Owen awoke to find his hands and feet tightly bound. He was sprawling in the clearing, against the wall of the cottage. Beside him lay Walton, similarly secured, and he saw that no great time had passed since their capture, for it was still dark, although in the east a faint gray light was beginning to pale the brilliance of the stars.

From where he lay he could see most of the clearing, and he noted the extraordinary activity there. The place swarmed with the plant-men, hurrying to and fro on enigmatic errands. A high, thin voice was directing their movements from the door of the cottage, and Owen squirmed into a position from which he could see the voice's owner. He looked, then shuddered with

deep loathing at the thing he saw.

It was Brilling that stood there, Brilling as Walton had described him, as the accelerating ray had left him. The enormous bald head, the dull white skin, the shapeless mass of flesh that was the body, with four twisting tentacles, on two of which it supported itself. As Owen stared at the monstrosity, it caught his gaze and came down toward the two. Standing in front of them, Brilling regarded the bound pair with mocking interest.

"So you came back, Walton?" he shrilled. "And you too, Owen. For what, I wonder!" And Brilling laughed, terribly.

Neither Owen nor Walton replied, and this seemed to enrage the monster before them.

"You came back in time to see my triumph," he raved, "the beginning of my reign." He scanned the eastern sky, then flung a muscled tentacle up in sudden exultation. "Look, you fools," he cried, pointing toward the east.

Both looked in that direction, toward the misty light of dawn, when something there caught their attention, something round and black that was drifting up into the sky from the distant eastern beaches. Up and up it floated, and now a far humming sound came to their ears, a purring whine that grew to a loud droning. As they watched, the first rays of sunlight struck the thing in the air and they saw it clearly. It was a vast globe of metal, a giant sphere that glinted dully in the sunlight. A huge globe all of a hundred feet in diameter, floating up into the sky like a weightless bubble.

The droning intensified, increased. Another of the round black shapes was floating up in the east, following the first.

And another, and still another, then a cluster of them, until all of fifty gigantic globes hovered a mile above the island's eastern side, circling, droning, massing.

Brilling turned to the two bound men, his face alight with evil triumph. "My armies!" he boasted. "My plant-men!" His eyes were glowing. "They go to spread death in your world, to sweep earth with the accelerating ray!" And even as he spoke, the two saw the globes moving slowly across the island, passing out in compact formation, high above.

His face upturned in the morning sunlight, Brilling watched them go. Owen turned toward his friend, then his heart leaped with sudden hope. For Walton was stealthily rubbing the ropes that bound his hands against a sharp edge of stone that projected from the ground beside him.

Owen saw that none of the plant-men remained in the clearing, that all had hurried away to the eastern beaches to watch the launching of the flying spheres. And he saw that Brilling was still intent on the massed globes above, which were now passing out from above the island out over the sea. From a corner of his eyes, without turning, he saw that Walton was fumbling at his footbonds, having freed his hands.

Brilling suddenly turned his attention toward the two prisoners. "And for you two," he resumed, "death!"

He turned and uttered a shrill call, a call that was echoed in the distance by a group of plant-men, returning toward the clearing. And even as he voiced that call, Walton had jumped to his feet and sprung, knocking Brilling to the ground, where the two rolled over and over, clutching and holding each other.

The four long tentacles coiled swiftly around Walton,

grasping him in an iron grip, and at the same time Brilling cried out again to the approaching plant-men, a hasty, shrill command that was instantly answered by the latter, whom Owen could see in the distance, racing toward the aid of their master. And a hundred feet across the clearing was the open door of the laboratory!

With a sudden convulsive movement, Owen rolled away from the cottage wall and out into the clearing, passing the struggling Walton and Brilling, working his way toward the open door that meant life or death for the world. A chorus of wailing shouts came to his ears as the plant-men sped toward the clearing, but Owen rolled on, all his being centered on that giant black cylinder inside the open door, and the switches on its front. And on a single switch, at the extreme left-hand side.

The left-hand switch! He was at the door now, had rolled inside and was madly striving to squirm into an upright position, against the great cylinder. Would his bonds baffle him, even now? As he flung himself to his feet with a supreme effort, he saw the plant-men race into the clearing, heard Brilling's command and saw them race past the struggling pair, toward the laboratory. They were coming—coming—

Leaning far over, Owen grasped the left-hand switch between his teeth. As he did so, the first of the plant-men raced into the laboratory, swung up one of the daggerlike flame-throwers toward him. But even as the deadly weapon was leveled full toward him, Owen had jerked down the switch between his teeth, by a quick movement of his head, snapping it wide open. For a fraction of a moment there was an utter silence.

Then, from outside, came a sudden wailing cry, faint and

fading. And as Owen stared, trembling, he saw the plant-men before him wavering, hesitating, saw their outlines soften, melt and change, seemed to glimpse them flashing through a thousand forms with lightning speed, then melt down to mere heaps of green slime, masses of green, slimy scum that smeared the floor and ground where the plant-men had stood.

Out beyond the open door, he saw Walton stagger to his feet, gazing in utter amazement at the heaps of slime around him. Then, reeling unsteadily into the laboratory, Walton had cut his bonds and the two walked out into the clearing, looking about as if unable to credit the miracle they had wrought.

Slime! Slime that lay where Brilling and the plant-men had moved a moment before, slime that lay wherever the plant-men had gathered. All life on the island, save for the shielded two, had sunk down to the first base of life, under the full power of the reversing ray, had flashed down to slime like that which covered the tidal beaches ages before.

Walton shouted, now, and pointed out toward the sea. The massed globes there, that had been speeding away from the island, were wavering, halting, driving about confusedly, the droning of their operation dying and ceasing, as one after another they plunged down into the sea, with great splashes. Spinning down into the sea, when the plant-men inside them were smitten down by the reaching, powerful ray. Smitten down—to slime!

The last of the flying globes splashed down and vanished, and Walton and Owen turned and looked at each other. There were tears standing in their eyes. Over the island lay a thick, stupendous silence.

6

As their little sailboat swept across the waters, Walton and Owen stood at its stern, watching the island drop behind. In the west, the setting sun hung at the water's edge, a great, flaming door into which the sea seemed to be pouring. And remembering the utter despair with which they had come down to the island so short a time before, Owen felt infinitely grateful, infinitely humbled.

Walton's thoughts were on something else. "Brilling gone," he said, "the plant-men all gone, the ray-projector destroyed by us—and I alone know how to make another."

"You are hardly likely to make another, are you?" asked Owen, smiling. But there was no smile on Walton's face as he answered.

"No, all that is finished, now. But it was close—close—"

As the two watched the island sink behind them, a silence fell on them, a silence of complete understanding. The sun had dropped down beneath the horizon, now, and they could hardly see the island in the darkening twilight. A moment longer they glimpsed it, a dark mass wavering against the distant skyline, then it had passed, had blended into the thickening dusk.

With a sigh, Owen turned around, and more slowly, Walton did likewise. Shoulder to shoulder, they looked out ahead. Thus the little yawl clove the waters, speeding steadily north through the swiftly gathering night.